# BIG-TIME
## HOCKEY RECORDS

Published by Capstone Press, an imprint of Capstone.
1710 Roe Crest Drive
North Mankato, Minnesota 56003
capstonepub.com

SPORTS ILLUSTRATED KIDS is a trademark of ABG-SI LLC. Used with permission.

Library of Congress Cataloging-in-Publication Data
Names: Berglund, Bruce R., author.
Title: Big-time hockey records / by Bruce Berglund.
Description: North Mankato, Minnesota : Capstone Press, 2022. | Series: Sports illustrated kids big-time records | Includes bibliographical references and index. | Audience: Ages 8–11 | Audience: Grades 4–6
Identifiers: LCCN 2021004282 (print) | LCCN 2021004283 (ebook) | ISBN 9781496695475 (hardcover) | ISBN 9781977159328 (paperback) | ISBN 9781977159038 (ebook PDF)
Subjects: LCSH: Hockey—Records—Juvenile literature.
Classification: LCC GV847.25 .B438 2022 (print) | LCC GV847.25 (ebook) | DDC 796.356—dc23
LC record available at https://lccn.loc.gov/2021004282
LC ebook record available at https://lccn.loc.gov/2021004283

Summary: Nothing beats the excitement of a player slapping the puck into the goal for a game-winning score—except when that big slap shot sets a new record! Behind every big-time hockey record is a dramatic story of how a player or team achieved greatness. Strap on your skates and read up on hockey's greatest players and teams and their historic record-setting performances on the ice.

Editorial Credits
Editor, Aaron Sautter; Designer, Bobbie Nuytten; Media Researcher, Morgan Walters; Production Specialist, Tori Abraham

Image Credits
Associated Press: Fred Jewell, 31; Getty Images: B Bennett, top 7, Focus On Sport, 55, Jamie Sabau, 51, Steve Russell, 5; Newscom: Chris Szagola/Cal Sport Media, bottom 7, Douglas R. Clifford/ZUMA Press, 35, Frank Jansky/Icon Sportswire DCT, 19, Gary Hershor/Reuters, 33, Josh Holmberg/Icon SMI 259, 40, Kostas Lymperopoulos/Cal Sport Media, 37, Michael Tureski/Icon Sportswire 147, 41, Philippe Bouchard/Icon Sportswir DC, 27, Sam Harrel/News-Miner/ZUMA Press, 29; Shutterstock: Pat Lauzon, 49; Sports Illustrated: Bob Rosato, bottom 30, Damian Strohmeyer, 10, David E. Klutho, 8, 21, 23, 25, 39, 43, 45, 57, 59Bottom of Form, Erick W. Rasco, 15, 42, Heinz Kluetmeier, 46, 47, 48, Manny Millan, 16, Neil Leifer, 13, Simon Bruty, Cover, 52, Tony Triolo, 9

All records and statistics in this book are current through the 2020–21 regular season.

# TABLE OF CONTENTS

WORDS IN **BOLD** APPEAR IN THE GLOSSARY.

# AN AMAZING GAME

It was the start of a new season in the National Hockey League (NHL). On October 12, 2016, the arena in Ottawa, Canada, was full of excited Senators fans. There were also hundreds of Maple Leafs fans who had made the trip from Toronto, Canada. Everybody was eager for hockey. What they didn't realize is that they would see a record broken that day.

Many fans had their eye on the Leafs' **rookie** player, Auston Matthews. Even though Matthews was only 19 years old, a lot of people expected him to be a star. He had played pro hockey in Switzerland the year before and was one of the leading goal-scorers. Now he was making his **debut** in the best league in the world.

Matthews scored his first goal midway through the first period, giving the Maple Leafs a 1–0 lead. A few minutes later, he **stickhandled** around four Senators players and put a brilliant shot past the goalie for goal number 2. Early in the second period, Matthews scored again for a **hat trick**. Then in the last seconds of the period, Matthews did something no NHL player had ever done before—he scored his fourth goal in his first pro game.

Maple Leafs fans roared. And although their team was losing, Senators fans also recognized that they'd seen something amazing.

Auston Matthews burst onto the scene when he scored 40 goals in his first NHL season.

Teemu Selänne holds the record for most goals in his first full NHL season. Playing for the Winnipeg Jets, Selänne scored 76 goals in his rookie season. He beat the old record by 23 goals!

Hockey has a long history. Even before lightbulbs were invented, people in Canada, the United States, and Europe strapped on skates to play on the ice with sticks and balls. The first game with a puck on an indoor rink took place in 1875 in Montreal, Canada.

The NHL got its start in 1917. From the very beginning, players were setting amazing records. In fact, some of the league's earliest records still stand today and might never be broken. For example, Montreal Canadiens goalie George Hainsworth set season records for most **shutouts** and lowest goals against average in 1928–29. It seems no goalie will ever come close to his records. Players today are faster skaters and more skilled with the puck. Today's goalies have a much harder job stopping shots than in Hainsworth's time.

Modern hockey players are top athletes. Players in both men's and women's leagues are strong, fast, and have amazing puck-handling skills. Their talents are what makes hockey an amazing sport and has led to amazing records.

## Most Goalie Shutouts, Career

| RANK | PLAYER | TEAMS | YEARS | SHUTOUTS |
|---|---|---|---|---|
| 1 | Martin Brodeur | New Jersey Devils, St. Louis Blues | 1991–2015 | 125 |
| 2 | Terry Sawchuk | Detroit Red Wings, Boston Bruins, Toronto Maple Leafs, Los Angeles Kings, New York Rangers | 1949–1970 | 103 |
| 3 | George Hainsworth | Montreal Canadiens, Toronto Maple Leafs | 1926–1937 | 94 |
| 4 | Glenn Hall | Detroit Red Wings, Chicago Blackhawks, St. Louis Blues | 1952–1971 | 84 |
| 5 | Jacques Plante | Montreal Canadiens, New York Rangers, St. Louis Blues, Toronto Maple Leafs, Boston Bruins | 1952–1973 | 82 |

## George Hainsworth
Winner of 1928–29 Vezina Trophy as NHL's best goalie
44 games, 22 shutouts, 0.92 goals against average

## Andrei Vasilevskiy
Winner of 2018–19 Vezina Trophy as NHL's best goalie
53 games, 6 shutouts, 2.55 goals against average

# Chapter One

# BIG-TIME SHOOTERS

## Streaking Stastny

After scoring four goals in his first game, Auston Matthews came back to earth. He didn't score any goals at all in his next game. In fact, there were several stretches in his rookie season when Matthews didn't record any goals or **assists** at all.

After his record-setting streak, Paul Stastny went into a slump. He went five straight games without getting a single point.

Sometimes even the best players go through slumps. They can't seem to get any shots on goal and their passes don't connect. But then there are those times when everything goes right one game after another.

Midway through his rookie season in 2006–07 with the Colorado Avalanche, Paul Stastny went on a record-setting streak. For six weeks, night after night, he scored goals and set up his teammates with assists. Stastny tallied at least one point per game for 20 games in a row. He ended up with 11 goals and 18 assists in those **consecutive** games. It was the longest points streak ever for a rookie.

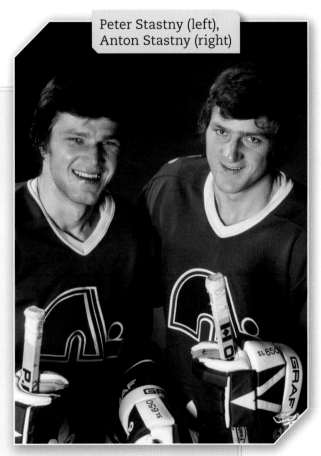

Peter Stastny (left), Anton Stastny (right)

### Like Father, Like Son

Paul Stastny's father, Peter, had a long NHL career. In his first season with the Quebec Nordiques, Peter Stastny broke the old record for most consecutive games with a point by a rookie. So once upon a time, Stastny the father held the record that is now held by Stastny the son. Peter Stastny was one of the NHL's top scorers during his career. For several years, he played on the same line with his two brothers, Anton and Marian.

## Overtime Master

There's little more exciting in hockey than games that go into overtime. Teams are allowed only three skaters, along with the goalie. Having fewer players speeds up the game and opens up more scoring chances. The teams fly back and forth across the rink, firing shots at the net. Fans are on the edge of their seats, hoping for their team to score first and win the game.

Alex Ovechkin has won more overtime games for his team than any other player. During his career, Ovechkin has scored the winning overtime goal 24 times. He also has assists on another 13 overtime goals for the Washington Capitals.

When games go to overtime, Alex Ovechkin (left) has led his team to more wins than any other player.

In 2020, Ovechkin scored his 700th career goal. He is only the eighth player in NHL history to pass that mark, joining all-time greats like Wayne Gretzky and Gordie Howe. But Ovechkin stands alone as hockey's clutch scorer.

## NHL 700+ Club

| RANK | PLAYER | TEAMS | YEARS PLAYED | GOALS |
|---|---|---|---|---|
| 1 | Wayne Gretzky | Edmonton Oilers, Los Angeles Kings, St. Louis Blues, New York Rangers | 1978–1999 | 894 |
| 2 | Gordie Howe | Detroit Red Wings, Hartford Whalers | 1946–1971, 1979–1980 | 801 |
| 3 | Jaromir Jagr | Pittsburgh Penguins, Washington Capitals, New York Rangers, Philadelphia Flyers, Dallas Stars, Boston Bruins, New Jersey Devils, Florida Panthers, Calgary Flames | 1990–2018 | 766 |
| 4 | Brett Hull | Calgary Flames, St. Louis Blues, Dallas Stars, Detroit Red Wings, Phoenix Coyotes | 1986–2006 | 741 |
| 5 | Marcel Dionne | Detroit Red Wings, Los Angeles Kings, New York Rangers | 1971–1989 | 731 |
| 6 | Alex Ovechkin | Washington Capitals | 2005–present | 730* |
| 7 | Phil Esposito | Chicago Blackhawks, Boston Bruins, New York Rangers | 1963–1981 | 717 |
| 8 | Mike Gartner | Washington Capitals, Minnesota North Stars, New York Rangers, Toronto Maple Leafs, Phoenix Coyotes | 1978–1998 | 708 |

*Stats listed are through the 2020–21 regular season.

## Offensive Defensemen

Players on defense aren't supposed to be big goal-scorers. They may occasionally score with a hard slap shot or set up a teammate on a goal. But their main job is to stop the other team. Defenders go after the puck and pass it ahead to the forwards.

But one amazing player changed that. Bobby Orr was a defenseman who played like a forward. Orr often skated around other players like they were standing still. He could rush from one end of the rink to the other, and then fire a shot past the goalie or pass to an open teammate.

Another NHL defenseman, Paul Coffey, scored more goals. But Orr holds the record for most assists and points by a defenseman in a season. Many fans feel that no other player was like Bobby Orr. He showed that even players on defense can change the game.

### Most Goals by a Defenseman in a Single Season

| RANK | PLAYER | TEAM | SEASON | GOALS |
|------|--------|------|--------|-------|
| 1 | Paul Coffey | Edmonton Oilers | 1985–1986 | 48 |
| 2 | Bobby Orr | Boston Bruins | 1974–1975 | 46 |
| 3 | Paul Coffey | Edmonton Oilers | 1983–1984 | 40 |
| 4 | Doug Wilson | Chicago Blackhawks | 1981–1982 | 39 |
| 5 | Paul Coffey | Edmonton Oilers | 1985–1985 | 37 |
| 5 | Bobby Orr | Boston Bruins | 1971–1972 | 37 |
| 5 | Bobby Orr | Boston Bruins | 1970–1971 | 37 |

A defenseman has totaled more than 100 points for the season only 14 times in NHL history. Bobby Orr did it six of those times.

Bobby Orr scored four goals and added four assists to help the Boston Bruins win the 1972 Stanley Cup Finals.

## Most Assists by a Defenseman in a Single Season

| RANK | PLAYER | TEAM | SEASON | ASSISTS |
|------|--------|------|--------|---------|
| 1 | Bobby Orr | Boston Bruins | 1970–1971 | 102 |
| 2 | Bobby Orr | Boston Bruins | 1973–1974 | 90 |
| 2 | Paul Coffey | Edmonton Oilers | 1985–1986 | 90 |
| 4 | Bobby Orr | Boston Bruins | 1974–1975 | 89 |
| 5 | Bobby Orr | Boston Bruins | 1969–1970 | 87 |

## Most Points by a Defenseman in a Single Season

| RANK | PLAYER | TEAM | SEASON | POINTS |
|------|--------|------|--------|--------|
| 1 | Bobby Orr | Boston Bruins | 1970–1971 | 139 |
| 2 | Paul Coffey | Edmonton Oilers | 1985–1986 | 138 |
| 3 | Bobby Orr | Boston Bruins | 1974–1975 | 135 |
| 4 | Paul Coffey | Edmonton Oilers | 1983–1984 | 126 |
| 5 | Bobby Orr | Boston Bruins | 1973–1974 | 122 |

# Top of Her Class

Hilary Knight knows about shooting the puck. At the 2018 NHL All-Stars Skills Competition, Knight put on a show in the shooting **accuracy** challenge. She hit all five targets in 11.64 seconds. That was more than four seconds faster than star Sidney Crosby.

Knight's fast, accurate shooting has helped Team USA in several **international** tournaments. Each year the U.S. Women's National Hockey Team plays in the world championships and the Four Nations Cup. And every four years, Team USA takes on the world's best teams in the Winter Olympics.

The U.S. Women's team's all-time top scorer in these tournaments is Hilary Knight. She has scored 117 goals for Team USA so far. And she's still scoring. She found the net three times against Team Canada in the 2020 Rivalry Series.

## Women's College Hockey Top Scorers

| RANK | PLAYER | TEAM | GOALS |
|:---:|:---:|:---:|:---:|
| 1 | Meghan Agosta | Mercyhurst University | 157 |
| 2 | Nicole Corriero | Harvard University | 150 |
| 3 | Hilary Knight | University of Wisconsin | 143 |
| 4 | Kendall Coyne | Northeastern University | 141 |
| 5 | Alex Carpenter | Boston College | 133 |

Since 2007 Hilary Knight (USA) has helped lead the U.S. Women's Hockey team to win 11 gold medals in the World Championships and Olympic Games.

Many women and men from Canada come to the United States to play college hockey. Meghan Agosta grew up in Ontario and played college hockey in Pennsylvania.

# Is the Great One the Greatest?

Hockey's most amazing scoring records belong to the Great One—Wayne Gretzky.

Before Gretzky came along, the record for most goals in a season was held by Phil Esposito. He scored 76 goals in the 1970–71 season. But the Great One blew past that in 1981–82 when he scored 92 goals. Before Gretzky, only Bobby Orr had more than 100 assists in a season. Orr did it once. Gretzky did it 11 times. And he's the only player to ever tally more than 200 points in a season. He achieved that feat four times.

Wayne Gretzky is called the Great One because he sits at the top of 61 NHL record lists.

There's no doubt that Gretzky was the greatest hockey player of all time. But how do his amazing records compare to other sports? Some sports fans have figured out how to compare records in different sports. First, they calculate how much better a record-setting athlete was compared to all other athletes in the same sport. The result is called the athlete's z-score. Then they compare athletes' z-scores in different sports.

When compared to record-setting players in other pro sports, Gretzky's z-score tops them all. The math doesn't lie. The Great One really is the greatest.

If you take away Gretzky's 894 career goals and count only his 1,963 assists, the Great One still has more points than the next player on the all-time list.

## Greatest Pro Athlete Z-Scores

| RANK | ATHLETE | SPORT | AMAZING RECORD | Z-SCORE |
|------|---------|-------|----------------|---------|
| 1 | Wayne Gretzky | Hockey | 2,857 career points | 4.6 |
| 2 | Pelé | Soccer | 1,280 career goals | 3.7 |
| 3 | Ty Cobb | Baseball | .367 career batting average | 3.6 |
| 4 | Michael Jordan | Basketball | 30.1 average points per game | 3.4 |

# BIG-TIME GOALIES

## Greatest Rookie Run

In January 2019, the St. Louis Blues had the worst record in the NHL. The team needed a fresh start to keep their playoff hopes alive. They decided to put in a new goalie, 25-year-old rookie Jordan Binnington. In his first start, Binnington completed a shutout against the Philadelphia Flyers. Binnington started 29 more games for the Blues and won 24 of them, including four more shutouts. St. Louis went from last place to the playoffs.

### Rookie Goalie Stanley Cup Winners

| PLAYER | TEAM | YEAR |
|---|---|---|
| Ken Dryden | Montreal Canadiens | 1971 |
| Patrick Roy | Montreal Canadiens | 1986 |
| Ron Hextall | Philadelphia Flyers | 1987 |
| Cam Ward | Carolina Hurricanes | 2006 |
| Matt Murray | Pittsburgh Penguins | 2016 |
| Jordan Binnington | St. Louis Blues | 2019 |

Before playing full-time for the St. Louis Blues, Binnington played several seasons with the Chicago Wolves in the American Hockey League (AHL).

Binnington stayed hot. The Blues surprised everyone by beating the Winnipeg Jets, Dallas Stars, and San Jose Sharks in the Western Conference playoffs. Thanks to their rookie's incredible play in the net, they made it to the Stanley Cup finals against the Boston Bruins. The two teams battled through the first six games to a 3–3 series tie. It would take Game 7 to decide who would lift the Cup.

In the final game, Binnington stopped 32 shots by the Bruins, and St. Louis won 4–1. The Blues' hot rookie goalie had started in all 26 playoff games and won 16 of them. It was the most playoff wins ever by a rookie goalie. But for Binnington, the last win was the most important one. The St. Louis Blues were Stanley Cup champs for the first time ever.

## "King" Henrik

Rookie goalies who win the Stanley Cup are very rare. So are goalies who win a lot of games year after year. The goalie who's been the most **consistent** over his career earned a worthy nickname—Henrik "The King" Lundqvist.

Henrik Lundqvist played pro hockey in his home country of Sweden before joining the New York Rangers. He also played for the Swedish national team at the world championships. When he started in the NHL, he already had a lot of experience against top players.

### Most Goalie Wins, Career

| RANK | PLAYER | TEAMS | YEARS PLAYED | WINS |
|---|---|---|---|---|
| 1 | Martin Brodeur | New Jersey Devils, St. Louis Blues | 1991–2015 | 691 |
| 2 | Patrick Roy | Montreal Canadiens, Toronto Maple Leafs, Colorado Avalanche | 1984–2003 | 551 |
| 3 | Marc-Andre Fleury | Pittsburgh Penguins, Vegas Golden Knights | 2003–present | 492* |
| 4 | Roberto Luongo | New York Islanders, Florida Panthers, Vancouver Canucks | 1999–2019 | 489 |
| 5 | Ed Belfour | Chicago Blackhawks, San Jose Sharks, Dallas Stars, Toronto Maple Leafs, Florida Panthers | 1988–2007 | 484 |
| 6 | Henrik Lundqvist | New York Rangers | 2005–present | 459* |

*Stats listed are through the 2020–21 regular season.

Henrik Lundqvist has been nominated five times for the Vezina Trophy, the award for the NHL's top goalie. He won it in 2012.

In his first season in 2005–06, "King" Henrik won 30 games for the Rangers. This began a record-setting streak. He went on to have seven straight seasons with 30 or more wins. No other NHL goalie has ever started his career with so much success. Lundqvist continued his winning ways and set another record by winning more than 20 games in 13 straight seasons.

Henrik Lundqvist played hockey in Sweden with his twin brother, Joel. One day at practice when they were 8 years old, their coach asked if anyone on the team wanted to play goalie. Joel lifted his brother's arm and said, "Henrik does." Many years later, Henrik and Joel played against each other in an NHL game.

# Racking Up the Wins

Goaltenders are a key part of a successful team. But even great goalies like Lundqvist can only do so much to help their teams win. The best teams each season don't just have a strong goalie. They also have solid defensemen and forwards that can score. The goalies who have the most wins for a season have one thing in common—they were surrounded by good teammates.

The New Jersey Devils' Martin Brodeur set a new record for most wins in a season in 2007. To do so, he played with a talented team that had won the Stanley Cup a few years earlier. In the 2015–16 season, Braden Holtby tied Brodeur's record. That year his team, the Washington Capitals, had the most wins of any NHL team.

But having a lot of wins doesn't guarantee a championship. Neither Brodeur nor Holtby won the Stanley Cup in the years they set the winning record. Even the best teams in the regular season can go cold in the playoffs.

## Most Goalie Wins in a Single Season

| RANK | GOALIE | TEAM | SEASON | WINS |
|------|--------|------|--------|------|
| 1 | Braden Holtby | Washington Capitals | 2015–16 | 48 |
| 1 | Martin Brodeur | New Jersey Devils | 2006–07 | 48 |
| 3 | Bernie Parent | Philadelphia Flyers | 1973–74 | 47 |
| 3 | Roberto Luongo | Vancouver Canucks | 2006–07 | 47 |
| 4 | Evgeni Nabokov | San Jose Sharks | 2007–08 | 46 |

Martin Brodeur (right) won the Vezina Trophy four times in his career.

# Career Savers

Hockey isn't like baseball. It doesn't have as many complicated **statistics**, such as a pitcher's true earned run average (tERA) or a batter's on-base plus slugging (OPS). With hockey, the main stats are goals, assists, wins, and shutouts. Those numbers usually tell you who the good players are.

But there is one important statistic used for comparing goalies: save percentage. To find out a goaltender's save percentage, you take the number of saves he makes in a game and divide that by the total number of shots on goal. So, if a goalie saw 30 shots in a game and saved 27 of them, the save percentage would be .900. That's pretty good.

The best goalies have a save percentage higher than .900. They are among the very best to play between the pipes. Dominik Hasek, Johnny Bower, and Ken Dryden are all in the Hockey Hall of Fame. Tuukka Rask is sure to join them when he finishes his career.

## Best Save Percentage, Career

| PLAYER | TEAMS | YEARS PLAYED | SAVE PERCENTAGE |
|---|---|---|---|
| Dominik Hasek | Chicago Blackhawks, Buffalo Sabres, Detroit Red Wings | 1990–2008 | .9223 |
| Johnny Bower | New York Rangers, Toronto Maple Leafs | 1953–1970 | .9219 |
| Tuukka Rask | Boston Bruins | 2007–present | .9215* |
| Ken Dryden | Montreal Canadiens | 1970–1979 | .9215 |
| Ben Bishop | St. Louis Blues, Ottawa Senators, Tampa Bay Lightning, Los Angeles Kings, Dallas Stars | 2008–present | .9205* |

*Stats listed are through the 2020–21 regular season.

Since becoming the Bruins' starting goalie, Tuukka Rask of Finland has been one of the best in the NHL. He has won the Stanley Cup once and the Vezina Trophy once.

# Chapter Three

# BIG-TIME PLAYOFFS AND STANLEY CUPS

## Canadien Domination

When pro teams win a league championship, they usually hang a banner or flag to celebrate. The Montreal Canadiens have put up more championship banners than any other NHL team. High above the ice at their home arena are 24 white banners, one for each of the Canadiens' Stanley Cup titles.

The Canadiens were the dominant team in the NHL during the 1950s and 1960s. Between 1951 and 1969, the team played in the Stanley Cup finals 15 times and won 10 of them. They also set a record during this stretch by winning the cup five years in a row.

The Canadiens kept up their winning ways in the 1970s. Led by goalie Ken Dryden, the team won six Stanley Cup titles, including four in a row.

Today NHL teams all have talented players. Teams are more evenly matched so that one team can't dominate the league for several years like the Canadiens did. It's unlikely any team will ever match or break the Canadiens' record of five consecutive championships.

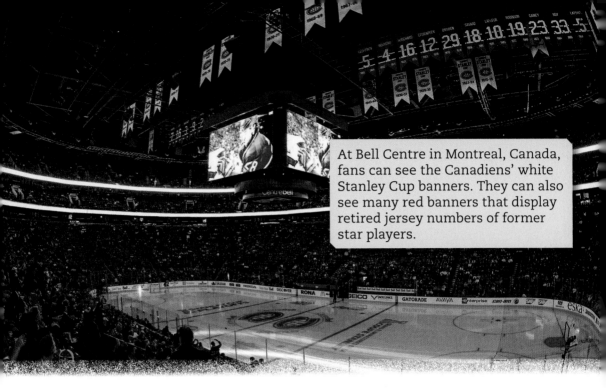

At Bell Centre in Montreal, Canada, fans can see the Canadiens' white Stanley Cup banners. They can also see many red banners that display retired jersey numbers of former star players.

## Most Stanley Cup Titles

| RANK | TEAM | CHAMPIONSHIPS |
|---|---|---|
| 1 | Montreal Canadiens | 24 |
| 2 | Toronto Maple Leafs | 13 |
| 3 | Detroit Red Wings | 11 |
| 4 | Boston Bruins | 6 |
| 4 | Chicago Blackhawks | 6 |
| 6 | Edmonton Oilers | 5 |
| 6 | Pittsburgh Penguins | 5 |

## Most Stanley Cup Losses

| RANK | TEAM | LOSSES |
|---|---|---|
| 1 | Boston Bruins | 14 |
| 2 | Detroit Red Wings | 13 |
| 3 | Montreal Canadiens | 9 |
| 4 | Toronto Maple Leafs | 8 |
| 5 | Chicago Blackhawks | 7 |
| 5 | New York Rangers | 7 |

# America's First Cup

In 1893 Lord Frederick Stanley was the representative for the Queen of England in Canada. He and his children were big fans of the new sport Canadians were playing—ice hockey. Lord Stanley was such a big fan that he bought a large silver bowl to be awarded to the best hockey team every year.

When Lord Stanley made his gift, he said it should be given to Canada's best hockey team. For the next 20 years, teams from Canadian cities and small towns played for Lord Stanley's Cup. But in 1914 a pro hockey league in western Canada began adding teams from the United States. The people who took care of the Cup said it should go to the world's best team, not just Canadian teams.

## Fastest Teams to Reach Stanley Cup Finals

| RANK | TEAM | YEAR | SEASON |
|------|------|------|--------|
| 1 | Vegas Golden Knights | 2018 | first season |
| 1 | St. Louis Blues | 1968 | first season |
| 3 | New York Rangers* | 1928 | second season |
| 4 | Boston Bruins | 1927 | third season |
| 4 | Florida Panthers | 1996 | third season |
| 6 | Edmonton Oilers | 1983 | fourth season |
| 7 | Buffalo Sabres | 1975 | fifth season |

*Won the Stanley Cup

The Seattle Metropolitans played in three Stanley Cup series between 1917 and 1920. The team won the title in 1917.

In 1917 the Seattle Metropolitans were the champions of the Pacific Coast Hockey Association. They defeated the Montreal Canadiens to become the first American team to win the Stanley Cup. There hasn't been a pro hockey team in Seattle since 1924. But beginning in the 2021–22 season, hockey fans there will have a new NHL team—the Kraken.

# Playoff Scoring Machines

The 1980s were particularly good for the Edmonton Oilers. Of the top six scorers in NHL playoff history, the Oilers can claim five: Wayne Gretzky, Mark Messier, Jari Kurri, Glenn Anderson, and Paul Coffey.

The 1980s Oilers teams were the highest-scoring in history. In one series during the 1985 playoffs, the Oilers scored an astonishing 44 goals in six games against the Chicago Blackhawks. In that same series, Oilers forward Jari Kurri set a new series record by scoring 12 goals. By the time the Oilers won the 1985 Stanley Cup, Gretzky had a new record for most points in the playoffs. In the Oilers' 18 playoff games that year, the Great One scored 17 goals and had an amazing 30 assists.

When looking at Wayne Gretzky's scoring records, fans often include only his goals, assists, and points during the regular season. But those numbers only tell part of the story. The Great Gretzky was also hockey's greatest playoff scorer.

Sidney Crosby and Evgeni Malkin are the NHL's current active playoff point leaders. Since becoming teammates in 2006, Crosby has 189 total playoff points (68 goals, 121 assists) and Malkin 169 (63 goals, 106 assists). They have led the Penguins to three Stanley Cup titles.

Wayne Gretzky (left) and Mark Messier (right) celebrated after the Edmonton Oilers defeated the Chicago Blackhawks in the 1985 Stanley Cup playoffs.

## Most Playoffs Points, Career

| RANK | PLAYER | PLAYOFF GAMES | GOALS | ASSISTS | POINTS |
|------|--------|---------------|-------|---------|--------|
| 1 | Wayne Gretzky | 208 | 122 | 260 | 382 |
| 2 | Mark Messier | 236 | 109 | 186 | 295 |
| 3 | Jari Kurri | 200 | 106 | 127 | 233 |
| 4 | Glenn Anderson | 225 | 93 | 121 | 214 |
| 5 | Jaromir Jagr | 208 | 78 | 123 | 201 |
| 6 | Paul Coffey | 194 | 59 | 137 | 196 |

# Longest Droughts

In 1995 the Quebec Nordiques moved to Denver, Colorado, and changed their name to the Colorado Avalanche. The move did wonders for the team. In the Avalanche's first season in Denver, the team won the Stanley Cup.

Hockey fans in Colorado didn't have to wait long to celebrate a championship. But fans in other cities have had to wait a long time. The worst Stanley Cup **drought** was a long 54 years. The New York Rangers won the Cup in 1940. But the team's fans had to wait until 1994 before celebrating another championship.

The Toronto Maple Leafs are close to beating the Rangers' record. The Leafs have won 13 Stanley Cup championships, which is the second most in NHL history. However, they haven't won it all since 1967.

## Teams with No Stanley Cup Titles

Arizona Coyotes

Buffalo Sabres

Columbus Blue Jackets

Florida Panthers

Minnesota Wild

Nashville Predators

Ottawa Senators

San Jose Sharks

Vancouver Canucks

Vegas Golden Knights

Winnipeg Jets

In 1994, Mark Messier (right) led the New York Rangers to their first Stanley Cup title in 54 years.

# Long Time, No Title

In the 2019 Western Conference Finals, the St. Louis Blues defeated the San Jose Sharks. Perhaps the most disappointed player on the ice was Sharks center Joe Thornton. During his long career, Thornton has had a lot of success. He's won the NHL's scoring title and was the league's 2005–06 Most Valuable Player (MVP). But he's never won a championship. While the Blues went on to win the Stanley Cup in 2019, Joe Thornton ended yet another season without lifting hockey's greatest trophy.

## Longest Active Players without a Stanley Cup Title*

| RANK | PLAYER | TEAMS | SEASONS |
|------|--------|-------|---------|
| 1 | Joe Thornton | Boston Bruins, San Jose Sharks | 22 seasons |
| 1 | Patrick Marleau | San Jose Sharks, Toronto Maple Leafs, Pittsburgh Penguins | 22 seasons |
| 3 | Brent Burns | Minnesota Wild, San Jose Sharks | 16 seasons |
| 4 | Zach Parise | New Jersey Devils, Minnesota Wild | 15 seasons |
| 4 | Henrik Lundqvist | New York Rangers | 15 seasons |
| 6 | Pekka Rinne | Nashville Predators | 14 seasons |
| 7 | Claude Giroux | Philadelphia Flyers | 13 seasons |
| 7 | Carey Price | Montreal Canadiens | 13 seasons |
| 9 | Erik Karlsson | Ottawa Senators, San Jose Sharks | 11 seasons |
| 9 | John Tavares | New York Islanders, Toronto Maple Leafs | 11 seasons |

*Stats listed are through the 2019–20 season.

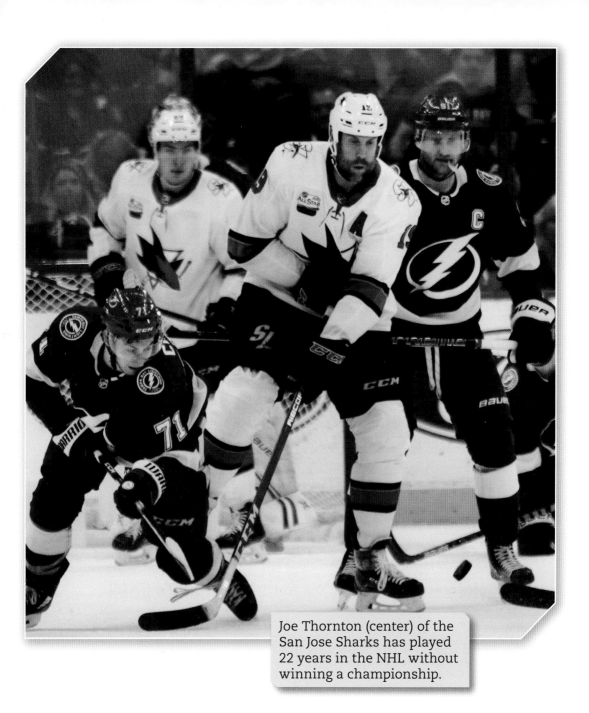

Joe Thornton (center) of the San Jose Sharks has played 22 years in the NHL without winning a championship.

# HOCKEY'S GREATEST TEAMS

## The Original Six

From 1942 to 1967, the National Hockey League had only six teams. These included the Boston Bruins, Chicago Blackhawks, Detroit Red Wings, Montreal Canadiens, New York Rangers, and Toronto Maple Leafs. These teams are now called the "Original Six."

Only two of these teams are original members of the NHL. Montreal and Toronto were both founding members of the league when it began in 1917. The other teams started a few years later.

The Montreal Canadiens are the NHL's oldest team. In fact, the team is even older than the NHL itself. The Canadiens played their first game on January 5, 1910. The team was a founding member of the National Hockey Association, which later became the NHL.

### How Old Are the Original Six?

1910—Montreal Canadiens begin playing

1912—Sinking of the *Titanic*

1914—World War I begins

1917—NHL is formed; Toronto begins playing

1924—Bruins begin playing

1926—Blackhawks, Rangers, and Red Wings begin playing

Jerseys from the NHL's Original Six teams were on display during the 2013 Stanley Cup Playoffs in front of Madison Square Garden in Manhattan, New York.

## Original Six Wins and Losses

The Original Six are the oldest teams in the league. They've won and lost more games than any other NHL team.

### Most All-Time Wins*

| TEAM | WINS |
|---|---|
| Montreal Canadiens | 3,473 |
| Boston Bruins | 3,241 |
| Toronto Maple Leafs | 3,000 |
| Detroit Red Wings | 2,989 |
| New York Rangers | 2,883 |
| Chicago Blackhawks | 2,812 |

### Most All-Time Losses*

| TEAM | LOSSES |
|---|---|
| Toronto Maple Leafs | 2,829 |
| Chicago Blackhawks | 2,761 |
| New York Rangers | 2,716 |
| Detroit Red Wings | 2,574 |
| Boston Bruins | 2,403 |
| Montreal Canadiens | 2,302 |

*Stats listed are through the 2020–21 season.

## Expanding the League

In 1967 the NHL added six new teams to the Original Six. This was the league's first **expansion**. Since then, it has expanded several more times.

Four of the 1967 expansion teams are still in the same city with the same name—the Philadelphia Flyers, Pittsburgh Penguins, St. Louis Blues, and Los Angeles Kings. One team, the Minnesota North Stars, moved to Texas to become the Dallas Stars. The sixth team, the California Golden Seals, went out of business in 1978.

The Flyers became the first expansion team to win the Stanley Cup in 1974. The Flyers have some of the most dedicated fans in the NHL. The team always ranks near the top in game attendance and jersey sales.

### Most All-Time Wins, Expansion Teams*

| RANK | TEAM | WINS |
|------|------|------|
| 1 | Philadelphia Flyers | 2,079 |
| 2 | St. Louis Blues | 1,929 |
| 3 | Pittsburgh Penguins | 1,903 |
| 4 | Dallas Stars | 1,842 |
| 5 | Buffalo Sabres | 1,805 |

*Stats listed are through the 2020–21 season.

### Most All-Time Losses, Expansion Teams*

| RANK | TEAM | LOSSES |
|------|------|--------|
| 1 | Los Angeles Kings | 1,828 |
| 2 | Vancouver Canucks | 1,746 |
| 3 | Pittsburgh Penguins | 1,734 |
| 4 | Dallas Stars | 1,708 |
| 5 | St. Louis Blues | 1,645 |

*Stats listed are through the 2020–21 season.

After joining the NHL in 1967, the Kings had a lot of losing seasons. In recent years, they have been one of the league's best teams. Led by Slovenian forward Anze Kopitar, the Kings won the Stanley Cup in 2012 and 2014.

# Best NCAA Men's Hockey Teams

Hockey fans don't just cheer for teams in the NHL. They also love to follow hockey in the National Collegiate Athletic Association (NCAA). In places like New Hampshire, Nebraska, and North Dakota, college hockey games draw thousands of fans.

Each year, the top college teams in the country play in the NCAA's Frozen Four tournament to decide on a national champion. The team that's won the most national championships in men's college hockey is the University of Michigan Wolverines. Michigan won its first title in 1948. The team went on to win five of the next eight championships. The Wolverines top the list of NCAA champions with a total of nine titles.

Max Pacioretty played with the University of Michigan Wolverines for only one season. The Canadiens were so impressed that they chose him in the first round of the 2007 NHL Draft.

## Most NCAA Division I Men's Hockey Championships

| RANK | TEAM | CHAMPIONSHIPS |
|------|------|---------------|
| 1 | University of Michigan Wolverines | 9 |
| 2 | Denver University Pioneers | 8 |
| 2 | University of North Dakota Fighting Hawks | 8 |
| 4 | University of Wisconsin Badgers | 6 |
| 5 | Boston College Eagles | 5 |
| 5 | Boston University Terriers | 5 |
| 5 | University of Minnesota Golden Gophers | 5 |

Each year, the top player in men's college hockey receives the Hobey Baker Award. Jack Eichel won the award in 2015 when he played with Boston University. He joined the Buffalo Sabres later that year. Many other winners of the Hobey Baker Award have also become stars in the NHL.

## College Teams with Most Hobey Baker Award Winners

| RANK | TEAM | AWARD WINNERS |
|:---:|:---:|:---:|
| 1 | University of Minnesota-Duluth Bulldogs | 6 |
| 2 | Harvard University Crimson | 4 |
| 2 | University of Minnesota Golden Gophers | 4 |
| 4 | Boston College Eagles | 3 |
| 4 | Boston University Terriers | 3 |

# Best NCAA Women's Hockey Teams

NCAA women's hockey features the best young players from the United States, Canada, and Europe. Many of the top women players in the Olympics, from many different countries, played college hockey in America.

### Most NCAA Division I Women's Hockey Championships

| RANK | TEAM | CHAMPIONSHIPS |
|:---:|:---:|:---:|
| 1 | University of Minnesota Golden Gophers | 6 |
| 1 | University of Wisconsin Badgers | 6 |
| 3 | University of Minnesota-Duluth Bulldogs | 5 |
| 4 | Clarkson University Golden Knights | 3 |

Hannah Brandt helped lead the University of Minnesota to win NCAA championships in 2013 and 2015. She then joined Team USA and has won five gold medals in the Winter Olympics and World Championships.

Minnesota has more young women playing hockey than any other state. It's no surprise that colleges in Minnesota have won the most women's hockey national championships. But great female hockey players come from across the United States.

Each season, the top player in women's college hockey receives the Patty Kazmaier Award. Julie Chu won the award in 2007 when she played for Harvard University. Chu holds the record with 196 career assists in women's college hockey. She also played for Team USA four times in the Winter Olympics.

# Chapter Five

# HOCKEY'S BIGGEST GAMES

## Hockey's Biggest Crowd

On December 11, 2010, more than 104,000 people filled the University of Michigan's football stadium. The Wolverines men's hockey team was taking on one of their rivals—the Michigan State Spartans. The largest arenas hold about 20,000 fans. But that day the huge crowd set a record for most fans at an outdoor game.

Teams began playing special games in outdoor stadiums in the early 2000s. The Wolverines and Spartans played at Michigan State's football stadium in 2001 in front of more than 74,000 fans. The NHL held its first outdoor game two years later. Over 57,000 people watched the Canadiens beat the Oilers in Edmonton. Fans had to bundle up to stay warm. The temperature was minus 7 degrees Fahrenheit (minus 21.7 degrees Celsius.)

Outdoor games are now a regular event in the NHL and college hockey. Hockey fans love watching the fast action on the ice on brisk winter days.

> Michigan Stadium is one of the largest football stadiums in America. Its nickname is the "Big House." So the hockey game between Michigan and Michigan State was called the "Big Chill in the Big House."

The 2003 Heritage Classic was the first NHL regular season game ever held outdoors. It was played at Commonwealth Stadium in Edmonton, Canada, between the Oilers and the Canadiens. More than 57,000 fans attended the game.

## Largest Outdoor NHL Games

| STADIUM | SCORE | DATE | ATTENDANCE |
|---|---|---|---|
| Michigan Stadium Ann Arbor, Michigan | Maple Leafs 3, Red Wings 2 | January 1, 2014 | 105,491 |
| Cotton Bowl Dallas, Texas | Stars 4, Predators 2 | January 1, 2020 | 85,630 |
| Notre Dame Stadium Notre Dame, Indiana | Bruins 4, Blackhawks 2 | January 1, 2019 | 76,126 |
| Ralph Wilson Stadium Orchard Park, New York | Penguins 2, Sabres 1 | January 1, 2008 | 71,217 |
| Levi's Stadium Santa Clara, California | Kings 2, Sharks 1 | February 21, 2015 | 70,205 |

## Hockey's Biggest TV Audience

The U.S. Olympic hockey team's victory over the Soviet Union at the 1980 winter games is one of the greatest upsets in sports history. The year before, the Soviets had trounced a team of NHL All-Stars 6–0. In 1980, Team USA was made up of young college players. Nobody thought the **underdogs** had a chance against the powerful Soviet team.

Despite the odds, Team USA defeated the Soviets 4–3. The team celebrated together on the ice while the fans in the arena went crazy. But nobody was watching on TV. The "Miracle on Ice" happened in the afternoon when most people were still at work or school.

Team USA stunned the world by defeating the powerful Soviet hockey team to advance to the gold medal round in the 1980 Winter Olympics.

After the game was over, news quickly spread across the country that the U.S. hockey team had won. A lot of people wanted to see how the Americans beat the Soviets, even those who had never watched a hockey game before. When the game was shown on TV that night, more than 34 million Americans tuned in to watch. To this day, the "Miracle on Ice" still holds the record for the largest TV audience ever for a hockey game.

After beating the Soviet Union, the U.S. Olympic team had to play one more game to win the gold medal. When the Americans beat Finland two days later, over 32 million people watched the game. This time the TV network showed it live.

# Huge High School Hockey

The Minnesota State Boys High School Hockey Tournament is the biggest and most popular high school hockey tournament in the United States. Some say it's the most popular high school tournament in any sport.

More than 250 Minnesota high schools have boys' hockey teams, more than in any other state. Only 16 teams make the state tournament. Some games are played in Xcel Energy Center, the home of the Minnesota Wild. Over 19,000 fans fill the arena to watch high school hockey. That's more people than go to many NHL games.

Herb Brooks had coached Team USA in the "Miracle on Ice." He had also coached college teams to win NCAA national championships and had coached in the NHL. As a young man he had even played in the Olympics. Someone once asked Brooks what the greatest thrill was in his career. "Of all the thrills I've had in hockey. . ." he said, "I can honestly say the biggest was winning the Minnesota State High School Hockey Tournament. No question about it."

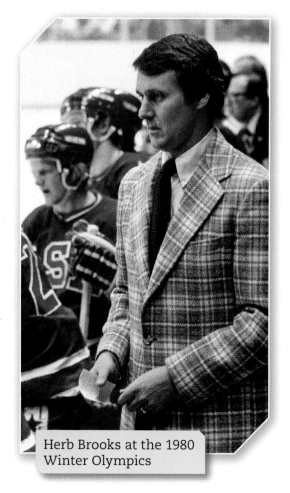

Herb Brooks at the 1980 Winter Olympics

## One Huge Crowd

Each year, the Quebec International Pee-Wee Tournament features more than 100 teams from around the world. Teams travel from as far away as Japan and Australia. Games are played over 12 days at Quebec City's Videotron Centre, which has more than 18,000 seats. In 2016 the tournament set a total attendance record with 236,000 fans.

The Minnesota high school tournament showcases the state's top 16 teams playing over four days in two classes. The record for biggest total attendance at a single tournament was 135,618 in 2015.

# FASTEST, STRONGEST, BIGGEST, SMALLEST

## Blazing Speed

The NHL's All-Star Weekend is one of the most exciting events of the year. A highlight of the weekend is the All-Star Skills Competition. The best players in the world compete against each other in events that test their shooting, passing, skating, and goaltending skills.

One event is the fastest skater contest. Each skater starts at the red line and makes one full lap of the rink, behind the nets. The fastest time wins.

### Fastest Woman on Skates

At the 2019 All-Star Skills Competition, Kendall Coyne Schofield set the mark for other players to beat. A member of the U.S. women's national team, she circled the rink in 14.346 seconds. Her top speed was 24 miles (38.6 kilometers) per hour.

Jonathan Drouin stunned everyone with the fastest time ever recorded at the 2015 NHL All-Star Skills Competition.

Players have been competing in the fastest skater contest since 1992. Some of the past winners are now in the Hockey Hall of Fame. But the all-time record for fastest time is held by a current player, Montreal Canadiens winger Jonathan Drouin. He skated a full lap in just 13.103 seconds.

Although Jonathan Drouin has the record for fastest time, most NHL players agree that the league's fastest skater is Edmonton Oilers center Connor McDavid. He won the fastest skater contest a record three years in a row and barely missed his fourth win in 2020.

## Hockey's Hardest Shooter

Another event in the NHL All-Stars Skills Competition is the hardest shot contest. Each contestant skates up to the puck and takes a slap shot into the net. A radar gun measures how fast the puck is flying. Several players are able to fire shots faster than 100 mph (161 kph). Defenseman Zdeno Chara holds the record for the fastest shot ever to win the NHL skills competition. In 2012 he launched a rocket that hit the net at 108.8 mph (175.1 kph).

While playing for the Boston Bruins, defenseman Zdeno Chara won the hardest shot contest a record five years in a row.

# Biggest and Smallest NHL Players

Today's average NHL player is more than 6 feet (183 centimeters) tall and weighs more than 200 pounds (91 kilograms). At 6 feet, 9 inches (205.7 cm) tall, veteran defenseman Zdeno Chara towers over anyone who's ever played in the NHL.

## NHL's Tallest Current Player

**Zdeno Chara**, Washington Capitals

6 feet, 9 inches (205.7 cm)

## NHL's Shortest Current Player

**Rocco Grimaldi**, Nashville Predators

5 feet, 6 inches (167.6 cm)

## NHL's Shortest Player Record

**Roy Worters**, Pittsburgh Pirates, New York Americans, Montreal Canadiens

5 feet, 3 inches (160 cm)

# Chapter Seven

# THE WORLD OF HOCKEY

## Worldwide Appeal

In several ways, the NHL is a global league. NHL teams have fans around the world. Teams also feature star players from many countries. About one-third of the league's players come from countries other than Canada and the United States.

The country with the most international players in the NHL is Sweden. Ulf Sterner was the first Swedish player in the league. He joined the New York Rangers in 1965, but he played only one season. At the time, most NHL coaches didn't think Swedish players were tough enough to handle the league's hard-hitting style of play.

Then defenseman Borje Salming joined the Maple Leafs. In his first game, he impressed the league by checking players into the boards and blocking shots with his body. He showed that Swedish players could play in the rough NHL.

Today, Swedish players are known for being big, fast, and skilled. They can dig the puck out of the corners, fly down the ice, handle the puck, and take powerful shots.

Borje Salming of Sweden played for 17 years in the NHL.

## Countries with the Most NHL Players

In 2020–21, NHL players came from 15 countries other than Canada and the USA. These countries had the most players in the league.

| RANK | COUNTRY | | NUMBER OF PLAYERS |
|---|---|---|---|
| 1 | | Sweden | 98 |
| 2 | | Finland | 60 |
| 3 | | Russia | 52 |
| 4 | | Czech Republic | 34 |
| 5 | | Switzerland | 12 |

# Champion Women

Every four years, the best national men's and women's hockey teams compete for the Olympic gold medal. The national teams also compete each year for the world championship title.

Team Canada and Team USA have been the two powerhouses in women's hockey. The Winter Olympics has featured women's hockey six times. Of those, the Canadian and U.S. women's teams have played each other in five gold-medal games. There have also been 19 world championship tournaments in women's hockey. Teams USA and Canada have faced each other in all but one of the 19 title games.

## Olympic Women's Hockey

| COUNTRY | GOLD | SILVER | BRONZE |
|---|---|---|---|
| Canada | 4 | 2 | 0 |
| USA | 2 | 3 | 1 |
| Sweden | 0 | 1 | 1 |
| Finland | 0 | 0 | 3 |
| Switzerland | 0 | 0 | 1 |

## Women's Hockey World Championships

| COUNTRY | GOLD | SILVER | BRONZE |
|---|---|---|---|
| Canada | 10 | 8 | 1 |
| USA | 9 | 10 | 0 |
| Finland | 0 | 1 | 12 |

Team Canada celebrated with Canadian flags and fans after defeating Team USA to win the gold medal in the 2010 Winter Olympics.

Some say that the rivalry between Canada and the USA in women's hockey is one of the best in all of sports. So far, Canada has edged out Team USA for more total championships.

# International Champs

Hockey is the national sport of Canada. It makes sense. The game was invented in Canada. For a long time, Canadian men were the best hockey players in the world.

Men's hockey was first played at the Olympics in 1920. Canada won the gold medal in that first tournament. At the 1924 Olympics, Team Canada was so dominant that they outscored their opponents 132–3.

In the 1950s a new hockey power challenged the Canadians. The Soviet Union beat Canada for the world championship in 1954. They soon became the best team in international hockey. From 1954 to 1991, the Soviet team won almost every world championship and Olympics.

The Soviet Union no longer exists. But Russia carries on its tradition of great hockey. Canada also still has one of the best teams in men's hockey. Other countries boast talented hockey teams, such as Finland, Sweden, and the Czech Republic. But you can always count on Canada and Russia to challenge for the championship.

## Olympic Men's Hockey

| COUNTRY | GOLD | SILVER | BRONZE |
|---|---|---|---|
| Canada | 9 | 4 | 3 |
| Soviet Union/Russia | 9 | 1 | 1 |
| USA | 2 | 8 | 1 |
| Sweden | 2 | 3 | 4 |
| Czechoslovakia/ Czech Republic | 1 | 4 | 5 |

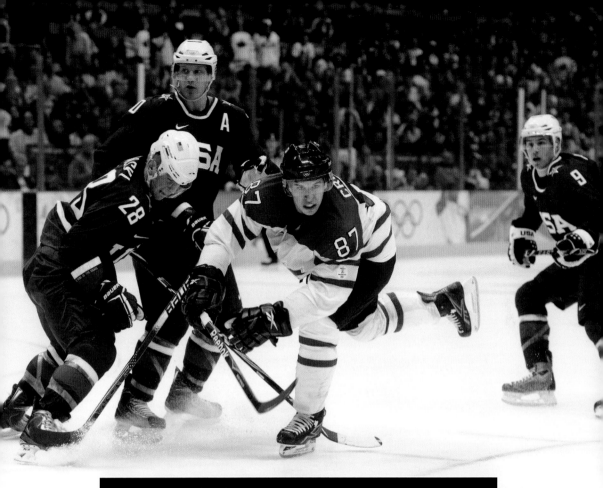

Sidney Crosby (#87) isn't just a star player for the Pittsburgh Penguins. He also plays for Team Canada. At the 2010 Olympics in Vancouver, Canada, Crosby scored an overtime goal against the USA to win the gold medal. It is remembered as one of the greatest goals in Canadian hockey.

## Men's Hockey World Championships

| COUNTRY | GOLD | SILVER | BRONZE |
|---|---|---|---|
| Soviet Union/Russia | 27 | 10 | 10 |
| Canada | 26 | 15 | 9 |
| Czechoslovakia/ Czech Republic | 11 | 13 | 20 |
| Sweden | 11 | 18 | 17 |
| Finland | 3 | 8 | 3 |

# BIG-TIME MOMENTS IN HOCKEY

## 1875
First hockey game played on an indoor rink with a puck

## 1892
Lord Stanley donates a trophy to be awarded
to the best hockey team in Canada

## 1910
The Montreal Canadiens play their first game

## 1917
The National Hockey League is created

## 1920
Hockey is played at the Olympics for first time

## 1924
Boston Bruins are first American team to join the NHL

## 1929
George Hainsworth sets goaltending
records and wins Vezina Trophy

## 1942
The NHL shrinks to 6 teams

## 1954
The Soviet national hockey team
wins its first world championship

## 1960
Canadiens win their fifth consecutive Stanley Cup

## 1967

The NHL adds six new expansion teams

## 1971

Bobby Orr is first defenseman
to record more than 100 points

## 1980

Team USA beats Soviets in
"Miracle on Ice" at the Olympics

## 1985

Edmonton Oilers win Stanley Cup and
set records for playoff scoring

## 1998

Women's hockey is featured in
the Olympics for first time

## 1999

Wayne Gretzky ends career as
hockey's all-time greatest scorer

## 2001

First championship in women's college hockey

## 2010

Canadian men's and women's teams both
win gold at Vancouver Winter Olympics

## 2019

Jordan Binnington leads St. Louis Blues
to win first Stanley Cup title

# GLOSSARY

**accuracy** (AK-yer-uh-see)—the ability to aim at something precisely and hit it

**assist** (uh-SIST)—a pass that leads to a score by a teammate

**consecutive** (kuhn-SEK-yuh-tiv)—when something happens several times in a row without a break

**consistent** (kuhn-SIS-tuhnt)—doing something in the same way time after time

**debut** (day-BYOO)—an athlete's first game at the pro level

**drought** (DROUT)—a long period of time when a player or team has little success

**expansion** (ik-SPAN-shuhn)—when a sports league adds more teams

**hat trick** (HAT TRIK)—when a hockey player scores three goals in one game

**international** (in-tur-NASH-uh-nuhl)—including more than one nation

**rookie** (RUK-ee)—a first-year player

**shutout** (SHUHT-out)—a game in which a goalie keeps an opposing team from scoring any goals

**statistics** (stuh-TIS-tiks)—a collection of data used to judge a player's or team's performance

**stickhandle** (STIK-hand-uhl)—to control or move a hockey puck with a lot of skill

**underdog** (UHN-der-dawg)—a team or player that is expected to lose a game or tournament

# READ MORE

Frederick, Shane. *Pro Hockey Records: A Guide for Every Fan.* North Mankato, MN: Capstone Press, 2019.

Keppeler, Eric. *The Greatest Hockey Players of All Time.* New York: Gareth Stevens Publishing, 2019.

Rule, Heather. *Wayne Gretzky and the Edmonton Oilers.* Minneapolis: Abdo Publishing, 2019.

# INTERNET SITES

*NHL Leaders and Records*
hockey-reference.com/leaders/

*NHL Records*
records.nhl.com/

*Sports Illustrated Kids*
sikids.com

# INDEX